Anonymous

**Buckland Centennial, September 10, 1879**

addresses, poems, songs

Anonymous

**Buckland Centennial, September 10, 1879**
*addresses, poems, songs*

ISBN/EAN: 9783337264505

Printed in Europe, USA, Canada, Australia, Japan

Cover: Foto ©Andreas Hilbeck / pixelio.de

More available books at **www.hansebooks.com**

# BUCKLAND CENTENNIAL,

## September 10, 1879.

—o—

## ADDRESSES, POEMS, SONGS, &c.

The celebration of Buckland's Centennial on Wednesday, Sept. 10, 1879, will long be remembered as one of the most pleasant occasions in the history of Franklin county. The day dawned beautiful after a night of clouds and storm, and thus contributed in no small degree to the grand success. Although no appropriation to defray the expenses of the Centennial had been made by the town, interested citizens had taken the matter in hand, and had by their individual efforts arranged for a celebration becoming so important an event in its annals. The Committee who had the matter in charge were, Frederick Forbes, J. B. Frost, J. A. Richmond, G. K. Ward, R. W. Field.

The exercises were inaugurated about half past 9 in the morning by forming a column near the bridge in Shelburne Falls. It was headed by a squad of mounted police under Deputy Sheriff H. S. Swan; then followed the Shelburne Falls Band, Henry Sweet, leader; Chief Marshal, Frederick Forbes; Aids, Captain F. W. Merriam, E. C. Frost, E. J. Stockwell, A. W. Ward; the Greenleaf Guards, commanded by Lieut. T. Cronan. A cavalcade of citizens brought up the rear, and under the escort as above proceeded to Bowen's Grove, about three-quarters of a mile up the Deerfield river on the Buckland side. This grove is now owned by Joel Thayer, is surrounded by open fields, with the merry waters of the Deerfield close by and the green wooded hills of Coleraine looming up beyond. It was soon apparent that the good people were coming from all the country around, not only from the hills of Buckland and her neighboring towns, but from a distance as well. Among the latter were Prof. W. F. Sherwin, of Newark, N. J., once a Buckland boy and now famous in the musical world; Dr. Gardner Wilder, of Circleville, Ohio, Rev. Samuel W. Clark, of Holyoke, Samuel Tobey, of Michigan, and others, who desired to show their filial love for the old town by joining in the celebration. One of the guests of the day was Miss Julia Ward, the present Principal of Mount Holyoke Seminary, who sought in this way to pay a tribute to the memory of Mary Lyon, the founder of the Seminary and Buckland's most famous daughter. The longevity of Buckland people is proverbial, and among those present who had grown up with the town almost from its incorporation, were Moses Nelson, alluded to in the address of the orator of the day as the last pupil who was under the instruction of his mother, and who is now in his eighty-eighth year; Dea. Silas Trowbridge, who is now eighty-two; Luther Pratt, about eighty-three; Hiram Dodge, who lives just over the line in the "edge of Hawley," eighty; Andrew Butler, eighty-two; Ezra Sherwin, seventy-five; Miss Parney Brooks, eighty-two, and Mrs. Fanny Richmond, eighty-one. It is estimated that the gathering numbered upwards of three thousand people. A portion found room on the seats provided, but many sat upon the ground, forming a semi-circle about the speakers's stand, while others stood or sat in their vehicles on the borders of the throng. The people were finally called to order, and rising, under the direction of Prof. Sherwin sang "America" with true heartiness and fervor. Divine blessing was invoked by the Rev. Mr. Jagger, of Shelburne Falls. Capt. J. A. Richmond, the President of the Day, then made the following

## ADDRESS OF WELCOME.

The record of the century for the town of Buckland is finished. The clock of centuries has struck one,—its echoing peals yet float along our valleys and linger on our hill-tops. Under the lengthening shadows of the old we sweep into the new. Standing to-day upon the threshold of the young century, we would fain pierce the misty veil just before us, and read the prospectus. But the eye of man cannot penetrate the veil, the hand of man cannot turn the page. But we may look back, and review and live over the past scenes of the old.

We may look back to the time when the wild beast roamed at will over the length and breadth of this town; to the time when the ax of Naham Ward first awakened the echoes and startled the wild beasts in this unbroken wilderness; to the time when the first child was born; to the time when the first grave was dug; to the time when the church bell first awakened the echoes of these hills and valleys. For this we have gathered to-day, and assembled on the banks of the historic Deerfield, once the highway of the red man over the Hoosac Mountain to the Mohawk Valley, now the highway of the nation *under* the Hoosac Mountain, from the east to the west. We have gathered here to-day to live over and bid adieu to the old and hail the new. We are happy and proud to have with us here to-day some of the sons and daughters of Buckland, who went forth from amongst us to fill places assigned them by destiny in other parts of our common country. You have come back to us to-day, from the busy, hurrying city that your energy and talent have helped to build up. You come from the sunny South and from the granite hills of the North; you come from the shores of the sounding sea, and from the almost boundless and majestic-prairies of the west,—from wherever there is a demand for the exertions of vigorous and skillful men. In behalf of the present residents of Buckland I bid you welcome back to your native town, —back to the scenes of your childhood; back to these beautiful valleys and majestic hills; back to the banks of this beautiful river upon which you have stood in youth, and pondered and wondered if any mightier existed; back to all the hallowed recollections that cluster around childhood and youth, which stamped their impressions upon your character and through you upon the world; back to the cot where you were born; back to the graves of your fathers; back to the hearts of your townsmen, who have watched with pride the problem that you have been solving on the blackboard of the world. In the name of your native town I greet you and bid you welcome. But we turn sadly from these happy inspirations and pleasant recollections as we remember townsmen that will come back to us never again; but especially as we remember our sons and brothers who formed a part of that glorious band of patriots and martyrs who gave their lives for the honor of our town and the salvation of our country. We miss them to-day, although they may not have gained sounding titles or national distinction yet they gave their lives for their country. Greater love than this hath no man. Although marble monuments may not tell how they fought or where they fell, although many of them sleep in unknown graves, they are not forgotten. Could my voice reach their ears to-day, as they file out on the ramparts of the sky to see what we do here,

I would say to them : "Behold the fruits of your sacrifice, you died not in vain ; although unmarked yet your graves may be, somewhere in God's quarries yet hidden from view—somewhere in the uncut granite there is a monument for you." To friends, natives of other towns and states who have come here to-day to assist us by their encouraging presence, and we expect eloquent words, to make this day one of the happiest and proudest in the history of our town, whether you come from the north, the south, the east or the west, we extend to you a brother's hand and a brother's welcome.

As we shall hear from our honored and venerable former towns-man, the story of the rise and progress of our town, the story of the trials and privations of our fathers, of their energy and perse-verance in hewing for themselves homes from these forest hillsides ; as we look back through and beyond the century and see through what trials, privations, disappointments and dangers our fathers have brought our town, let us realize our obligations and endeavor to raise the standard to a higher plane than it now occupies. Let us at least on this glad Centennial day lay aside and forget all personal and petty animosities, if any exist, and unite to-day as a band of brothers, and endeavor to make this one page of our record, which will go down from generation to generation ; let us make it clean and bright, without a blot or an erasure.

Music was finely rendered by the band, then it was announced that Rev. W. A. Nichols, of Lake Forest, Ill., who had written an historical poem, which was to have been read at this time, was pre-vented from filling the engagement by reason of illness. He had been stopping for a few days with friends in Charlemont and had taken a sudden cold. He had sent a letter of regret, which was read by Hon. Henry Winn. Another poem, written by Mrs. Snow, of South Meriden, Ct., (formerly Miss Sophia P. Woodward, of Buckland,) which was to come later in the day, was read by Sena-tor Winn.

## Centennial Poem.

### BY SOPHIA P. SNOW.

One hundred years! How great the change
  They've wrought throughout the earth
Since that eventful Autumn day
  When Buckland had its birth.

Could we behold the town as then,
  What wonder and surprise
Would penetrate our inmost souls
  And flash from out our eyes.

The panther unmolested roamed
  With boldness through the wood,
While here and there in solitude
  A rude log cabin stood.

The deer climbed o'er these rocky hills
  And bounded through the glen,
While in the mountain's dark ravine
  The bear sought out his den.

The Indian once roamed through this vale
  With scalping knife and bow,

On some relentless errand bent
  Against the pale-faced foe.

No Sabbath bells were ever heard
  Upon that sacred morn:
The only signal of alarm,
  The shrill, resounding horn.

No magic wire had then been taught
  Its skillful part to play,
And Greenfield seemed almost as far
  As Canton does to-day.

The mode of traveling with the poor
  And those of high renown
Was after the John Gilpen style
  "Of famous London town."

The dashing brook, all unrestrained,
  Leaped down the craggy hill,
Nor dreamed that human hands had power
  To chain it at their will.

Old Deerfield waters, then as now,
  Swept onward soft and low;
September's sun shone just as bright
  One hundred years ago!

To-day how changed these hills and vales,
  How different is the scene;
Where once the mighty forests stood
  Rise landscapes fair and green.

The cabins of the olden times
  Have long since passed away;
With pleasant cottages our hills
  Are dotted o'er to-day.

The dashing brook long since has learned
  To yield to human will,
And meekly turns the noisy wheel
  Within the busy mill.

Instead of war-whoops, blasts of steam
  Resound this valley through,
And bridges spanned the rapid streams
  Where crossed the birch canoe.

The iron horse, with lightning speed,
  Goes thundering through the vale,
Where once the trees, with bark chipped off,
  Were made to mark the trail.

Where once the wild beast had its lair,
  And savage feet oft trod,
Our public schools in grandeur rise,
  Our church spires point to God!

Oh had these hills and vales a tongue,
  What mysteries they'd unfold,
What daring deeds they'd bring to light
  That never have been told.

Fair Clesson, could'st thou speak to-day,
  What wonders thou would'st tell,
What dangers that our fathers braved,
  What hardships them befell.

Say, did the red man roam thy banks,
  Fish in thy crystal flood,
And cause thy waters sweet and pure,
  To drink the white man's blood?

And did the dusky maiden then
  Roam by thy silver stream,
And dream as maidens now are wont,
  Love's sweet, enchanting dream?

Although 'tis known thou hast a mouth,
  Thou dost no secrets tell,
Except unto the Deerfield's ear,
  Who ever guards them well.

And since these hills and vales no light
  On Buckland's history cast,
We can but hope her future 'll be
  As prosperous as her past.

Her sons and daughters have gone forth
　To win for them a name;
Her Hons. and LL. Ds.
　Are not unknown to fame.

Her Taylors, Porters, Sherwins, Wards,
　Her Putnams, Smiths and Trows,
Her Grahams, Ballards, Forbes and Fields,
　Shall live till time shall close.

Nor ever, too, shall be forgot,
　Her Trowbridges, Townsleys, Thayers,
Her Butlers, Richmonds, Allis, Frost,
　Her Woodwards, Williams, Wares.

Her Griswold's and her Lyon's fame
　Will ever sacred be;
Her Cummings, Spaulding, Allen, Long,
　Still live in memory.

'Tis well to pause upon our way,
　Look back adown the years,
Review the scenes through which we've passed
　With all their smiles and tears.

We love to live again the days
　When we were blithe and young,
Tell stories that our parents told,
　And sing the songs they sung.

And now in our maturer years
　We love to live them o'er—
Those apple-parings, spelling schools
　We had in days of yore,

O, golden past! for happiest hours
　The palm is ever thine;
No days will ever be to us
　Like those of "Auld Lang Syne."

In later years our country's call
　For men to quell the strife
Was answered by our valiant sons,
　Who risked for her their life.

Their graves are scattered far and wide,
　Upon the Southern plain,
Throughout the valleys of the West,
　And by the roaring main.

Though absent from our ranks to-day,
　They who for freedom bled,
Let us devote a moment's time
　Unto our honored dead!

And thus, though dead, they speak to us
　In music's solemn strains;
Their memory ne'er shall be forgot
　As long as life remains.

And there are others, O, so dear,
　We cannot pass them by,
Although with meekly folded hands
　So silently they lie.

We saw them robed in snowy white,
　Borne out the homestead door;
Clods fall upon their coffin lids,
　And they were ours no more.

This festal day brings back our loss
　With all its old time power,
For were they living, would they not
　With us enjoy this hour?

And yet we would not wish them back,
　Life's ills to longer bear;
Eternal, not centennial, is
　Their celebration there!

Another hundred years, and we
　Who tread these haunts to-day,
With all our joys, our hopes and fears,
　Shall then have passed away.

But if our children's children then
　Are faithful to their trust,

They'll celebrate this day when we
  Lie mouldering in the dust.

Old Buckland! precious, honored name—
  We look on thee with pride;
Land where our infancy began,
  And where our fathers died.

No matter where thy children stray,
  Whate'er their lot may be,
Home of our birth, no spot on earth
  Can ever equal thee!

Next upon the programme came an original song by Prof. Sherwin, which he had written and composed for the occasion. He sang in excellent voice, and as the last refrain died away among the hills, the audience expressed their appreciation with hearty applause.

## The Days of Long Ago.

I'm thinking of the old times,
  The days of long ago,
When you and I were young, boys,
  With spirits all aglow.
We built our "castles in the air,"
  With many lofty towers,
And hope's bright rainbow spanned the schemes
  Of Childhood's dreamy hours.

*Refrain* —I'm thinking of the old friends,
      And singing of the old songs,
      And dreaming of the old times—
      The days of long ago.

I'm thinking of the old songs
  We sung in days of yore,
The melodies that linger
  In memory evermore!
From holy hymn or anthem grand,
  To home songs breathed at even—
Sweet preludes to the nobler songs
  And harmonies of heaven!

*Ref.*—

I'm thinking of the old friends
  Who gathered with us then,
From alto boys to patriarch
  Of three-score years and ten.
When hearts were linked in sacred bonds
  Of friendship strong and true,
In joy and sunshine, or when grief
  Its darkening shadow threw.

*Ref.*—

I'm thinking—yes, I'm thinking,
  Amid the olden scene,
The hills, the vales, the meadows,
  The same old village green;
Yet weird and plaintive melodies
  Are breathing through my soul,
And blending in a saddened tone
  Beyond the heart's control.

*Ref.*—

We sing to-day the old songs,
  But ah! the voices gone!
We meet to-day as old friends,
  But miss an absent throng!
God grant that in the Better-land
  Where they have gone before,
Old friends may meet, while love and song
  Flow on forevermore.

*Ref.*—

The orator of the day, Joseph Griswold, Esq., of Griswoldville, was now introduced as one of Buckland's boys who had discovered and utilized the power of one of the tributaries of the Deerfield, which was now turning 17,000 spindles. Mr. Griswold is seventy-five years old, but still possesses a clear head and all the fire and enthusiasm of his youth. For an hour and a half he held his audience in the closest attention, notwithstanding the fact that clouds gathered overhead and the rain-drops fell thickly upon the unsheltered people. He avoided the dry statistics usually compiled by orators for such occasions, and painted with the skill of a master, pictures of the olden time, and portraits of the fathers and mothers who had peopled the hills of Buckland. He uncorked a fund of traditions, stories and anecdotes which was apparently inexhaustible, and thus kept his hearers in merry humor from beginning to close.

## THE HISTORICAL ADDRESS.

Mr. President and Ladies and Gentlemen :—

Buckland was incorporated as a town April 14, 1779. We have assembled to-day to commemorate the centennial of that event. It is not exactly within my province to go farther back than this date, and I will simply state the little that is known of its earlier history. There seems to have been a gore of land lying between Ashfield and Charlemont, which before this incorporation and christening went by the name of "Notown." Grants had been made to the Wards in the west part, to the Wilders, Taylors and Carters in the center, and in the eastern section to the Johnsons and Spragues; but no exact dates can be discovered except that of a deed dated in 1771, to Captain Gardner Wilder of land bordered by Charlemont on the north, and Ashfield on the south and indefinitely east and west. It is claimed by some that it began to be settled as early as 1740–50, but as the birth of the first child is given in 1770, we cannot reconcile these statements. Our fathers did not wait twenty or thirty years before beginning on their large families; if it were in this generation we could more easily credit it.

Clessons river, running through the center and taking its rise in Hawley and Ashfield, was named by a mill owner near its source, and the town is presumed to have been called Buckland from the fact that Squire Samuel Taylor, the early pioneer had a deer-park between the mill-yard and the Deerfield river. I have myself seen some of the old hurdle fence, and can recollect hearing Mr. Taylor talk of this park. When the town was incorporated, the north line was pushed back to the Deerfield river, and the south to the Four-corners, the west to Hawley "No. 7," and east to Conway, making a town of about 16,000 acres.

It is proper for me to commence by saying that Buckland was born in the midst of the Revolutionary struggle and many were off to the battle field. It was a time of hardship and trouble; yet the hardy race of people who had already settled here founded families, who have grown up to honor the place of their birth and have filled positions of usefulness in all parts of this wide and rapidly growing country. When the war closed, poverty and the taxes made men discontented, and hence arose the Shays insurrection, which seemed at one time as though it would overthrow the State government. It is said that while the insurgents in this rebellion were stationed near Springfield, and in the midst of a revel, the order was given to disperse. This order being met with derision, a blank volley was fired, followed by another of balls over their heads. This producing no effect the balls were fired into the crowd, and a number fell. One of the Buckland boys, Don Sprague, said to his father, "Dad, do they fire balls here?" "To be sure," he replied, "what the devil do you suppose they fire, hasty-pudding?" Then Don started, and did not slack his speed till he found himself in Hog Hollow.

Time assuages everything; and a few years after the war, Buckland was an industrious and thriving town. It was interesting to hear these old Revolutionary soldiers relate their experiences. I knew most of them, and can well recollect their countenances and voices. They were a fine set of jolly old fellows, long since gone to their final rest; and when we of this generation pass away, their pleasant faces and jocund voices will live only in history; but the nation that they fought and laid down their lives for, let us hope, may long live and maintain the spirit of '76! Of those engaged in the war of 1812, a few now remain with us. In 1814, Buckland was called upon suddenly to send a draft of soldiers to Boston. On a Sunday morning (Daniel Webster said there were no Sundays in Revolutionary times) the candidates marched up to draw either blanks or prizes. Moses Nelson slowly came up, put in his hand and drew—a prize. Then all went to the meeting house to hear Mr. Spaulding, and I remember well how Moses' mother wept and cried because her boy had been drafted for the war. Capt. Mayhew used to tell of the jolly times they had in Boston, and how Moses became frightened at some of the city society they saw and started to run for the barracks, falling headlong down the stairs. I am inclined to ask Mr. Nelson, as he used to crack so many jokes on me, whether the pension he now gets is for the hurt of that fall, the cries of his weeping mother, or the fifteen days he spent idling in Boston?

Buckland had no soldiers, that I know of, stowed away in the Calcutta death hole or the Dartmoor prison, but Coleraine had several. In the late war, when brother fought brother and the country was filled with lamentation and blood, this town sent her full share, and many a household mourns to-day the lost ones who never returned. I am not going to harrow your feelings by expressing any opinion in regard to the late struggle; the time has not come for that. It will take a century from the close of the war to settle this question correctly in the light of history. I will only say that slavery is forever abolished on our soil, and we are a nation, and may God grant that we never drift into an empire. War is a terrible

2

calamity, and leaves in its train moral degradation and enormous taxes, but we hope we are slowly coming back to prosperity. The soldier has had enough of war, and is glad to return to the peaceable pursuits of life; once a year he rests from his labor; and how beautiful and appropriate it is for him to go and decorate the graves of his companions in arms, and in the revolving years his grave also willl be decorated.

And in our own homes we all mourn the absence of our lost ones. We open the drawer and look at the mementoes of those long passed away—of the girl just blooming into womanhood, the hope and joy of the mother; the mementoes are there; so is the aching void in the mother's bosom. Here are the mementoes of the boy ripening into manhood, the joy and pride of his father; the mementoes, the pictures are there; so is the void in the father's heart. We go into the yards and look at our beautiful flowers that loving hands have trained, and loving eyes have looked upon with pleasure; the flowers are there in all their beauty; but the smiling face, the hand that trained and plucked those flowers is not. Let us gather them freely, and with the wild flowers of the valley, let us go as the sun is seting and strew profusely the new-made grave.

At the time of this incorporation there was no such thing known in the wide world as steam power; no such thing known as spinning and weaving by machinery; no steamboats, no railroads—not even a pleasure carriage here: and as for family likenesses in which we so much delight at the present time, their photographs were little black profiles, cut by Ezra Wood, to hang around the chimney piece. I remember, as but yesterday, when the improvement was made in the wheel head of our mother's time, by having three whirs instead of one, so the girls could do three times as much work. How mothers rejoiced and sisters danced; but before the bearings were worn smooth machinery was invented to spin by water power, and the wheel heads were laid away in the garrets, where you may find some of them to-day.

About sixty-seven years ago the shakers brought the first corn brooms to Buckland. Before that, the brooms were peeled by the Brackets, the Perkins, blind Sam Carter, old Mr Negress, Butler, Temple, and many others, who used to carry them to the store on horseback, tied behind them, and sell for six to ten cents apiece.

Buckland had in those early days a very superior class of mechanics, especially workers in wood; Col. John Ames was the first, and was a prominent man when the town was incorporated. He built the first meeting house in 1794, and framed it by try-rule. His apprentices were Col. Howland of Conway, Col. Snow of Heath, Charles Pelton, Capt. Chandler Carter, his son John, and my father, who closed his apprenticeship with him in 1798. My father's apprentices were Elisha Smith, Simeon Wood, Lyman Wood, Josiah Ward, Asa Davis, Asa Ruddock, (who left out of health at twenty years of age and studied medicine) Edmund Cheney, A. Hathaway and three of his own sons; and then Mr. Smith had his own son, Mr. Frost, Mr. Pelton and others. The intelligent and capable joiner, now at Shelburne Falls, came down from this same tuition and I may say that to be a thoroughly good carpenter requires a sense of the fitness and proportion of things as well as skill in handiwork, and you have but to go to Griswoldville and see the street they have lately built up for us to prove that these workmen have both.

Then we had the old blacksmith, "Sir" Brooks, at the center, whose brother Jabez took his place and left his own by the Bachelor bridge. Afterward White and Philip Jones had this shop, and it was here Josiah Pratt made the first cast-steel axes he became so noted for. John Carter had a shop in the north part of the town and Amos Wood in the south part. There was also the old grist and saw-mill of Mr. White at the mill-yard, and another just below the present one near the Bachelor bridge, and then came the John Ward mills which had been previously owned by Uncle Jacob Whiting's father. I think some of us can remember going to this mill with three full bags and two empty ones, and when the grist was ground and packed on the horse, and Uncle John took the boy by collar and posterior, it was a pretty close shave whether the boy landed on the bags or on the ground.

At the Four-corners have been numerous shops and mills. It was here that Ezra Wood made so many shaving boxes and manufactured combs: Butler & Smith, augers, butts and gimlets; and myself, sash, doors and blinds. In the bend of the river above was the long-noted carding and dressing mill of Mr. Pomeroy, and every few rods up the stream was a mill site for turning, sawing, grinding, &c., till you come to the Upper City, and there, in the earliest of my recollections, were substantial mills for grinding, sawing, and, in point of fact, the west part of the town, sixty years ago, carried on the most business.

The account of the suffering and poverty that these early families endured would fill a volume for each; but I will speak particularly of but one, and this one the direct ancestor of so many of us present: Grandfather White was off for the war and grandmother was dying. She lifted up her eyes and exclaimed, "What will become of these four little motherless girls! I leave you in the hands of your Heavenly Father," and so died. Oh, the struggles and sorrows of poverty! They sewed and knit and carried to grandfather Nichols, who had land and sons but not daughters, and in return brought away a peck or half bushel of grain, which they carried on their backs to the mill. They studied by the light of pine knots—for there never was a White but would have learning, and one of them very early in life began to keep school, and I have heard her tell her experience in boarding around; how at the table the pie and the cake would be passed uncut, and the head of the family did not wish for any, of daughters the same, and what could the bashful girl teacher say? So she went to bed hungry and she lay cold. I am glad to be able to say that this was not in the first families of Buckland. These girls also did housework over the river, and to their latest days always spoke well of the Hawkses of Charlemont. The last school my mother kept was in 1799, near Buckland Common, where the old graveyard now is, and which building was afterward burned. Mr. Nelson is, so far as I know, the only living pupil of that school. She kept twenty-four weeks for fifty cents a week, and with her wages she bought for a wedding dress six yards of silk at two dollars a yard, and I have here a sample of the silk which is eighty years old. Who could foresee the destiny of those four little girls whom the dying mother gave back to their Maker? One of those motherless infants became the wife of Sir Brooks, one of Major Griswold, one of Lieutenant Hastings and one of Captain Booth. In the aggregate they gave to the world fifty-two children, and though the graveyard claimed its share, there is scarcely an old family in Buckland that is not connected either by blood or marriage ties;—the Wards, the Forbes, the Butlers, the Woods, the Pomeroys, the Brackets, the Frosts, the Pratts, the Peltons, the Smiths, the Davises, the Tobeys, the Perkins, the Richmonds, the Sherwins, the Taylors and Carters, the Grahams, the Putnams, the Townsleys and Wilders, the Ballards and Maynards, and hosts of others I do not now recall; and as the expanding wave rolls out the new comers are absorbed, the Trows, the Caswells and Warfields, the Johnsons, and the Spragues and the Wares, Samuel Taylor and his brother Lemuel, and Mr. Nichols married into the same blood, so it takes in the Longleys, the Mantors and Grouts of Hawley, and the Cooks of Ashfield. So over the river it connects with the Averys, the Ballards, the Leavitts, the Hawkses, and also Dr. Bates by intermarriage with the Hunts of Heath. These descendants and connections are to-day scattered from the extreme Pacific coast to the Gulf of Mexico, and along the Atlantic to the British possessions, and westward to the setting sun and the line of civilization,—so numerous that you cannot count them—yea, almost as the sands of the sea shore. At the close of this century it may be presumed that their blood will be flowing in the veins of a million of human beings. Well may I repeat, who can forecast what will be the future of little motherless girls when the dying mother gives them back to her God.

It may be expected that I should speak at some length of the politics and geography of this town, but I do not choose to do so. For those statistics I refer you to the "History of the Connecticut Valley," just published. The valuable records of Buckland were burned in your late fire, and though we know they had town meetings and political strifes and animosities, those old strifes are over and their conflicts ended, and it matters little to-day to them or to us, who was selectman or field driver in the different years. In the spring of 1780, it was said that the snow was so deep that old 'Squire Taylor, Capt. Gardner Wilder and Elias Carter alone turned out and adjourned the April meeting, and they reached there on snow shoes. The Taylors and Carters were prominent in town matters and the Sherwins, Bemans and Pratts in the church. Here were these hills and streams in our fathers' time and here they are to-day; they speak for themselves and need no compliments from me. But it is our ancestors, the early settlers, whose names and faces we would call up to-day. They are not here to speak for themselves, so let us talk a little about our old grandparents, how they looked and what they said and did —the good old fathers and mothers who built up this town and raised those large families. In those early times there were few books and fewer newspapers in our old homes. In our infancy we gathered around grandmother or aunt to hear the nursery tales. "What will we have for a story to-night?" "Oh, Kid and his master going over London bridge." Link by link she would add, and adding revolve back to the beginning, and for the hundredth time close by saying, "time kid and I were home an hour and a half ago," and we went to bed with pleasing dreams. The stalwart boys would go to hear old grandfather Ward tell stories—I mean the great grandfather of any Ward now living—but the girls were too timid to listen, and even brave boys would stop their ears and hurry home in the dark to get inside before the boogers caught them. I say we would go down to John Ward's, the miller that ground the rye meal that made the nice bread that our mothers kneeded and baked on the old oven bottom. Oh, that old rye bread that we grew upon! what would you give to-day, old white haired men and women, if you could have the old wooden bowl or pewter porringer, the old iron spoon filled with the same old rye bread and good new milk, and the same old appetite! Well, we would go down to hear grandfather Ward tell his marvelous stories, but would first stop in the kitchen to eat some of the nice apples Aunt Lois always had for us, and then file into Grandfather Ward's room. He was a nice old gentleman, well dried up and preserved; his limbs about the size of candle moulds, his tight pants stopped at his knees, where they were met by his long stockings and silver knee buckles. He also had buckles for his slippers. His vest was cut round, his hair powdered, and a nice old gentleman was he. Mrs. Ward was also a well-preserved old lady. She sat in the corner in a low rocking chair, bottomed by the blind Mr. Carter. Her dress was the tow and flax, woven in the plaid and stripe as our mothers wove them; apron and handkerchief the same, and cap of white check linen. She would rock and she would knit, and she would knit and she would rock, and occasionally lay down her knitting and take up the little box, put in her thumb and finger and take a pinch. We would sit around the fire-place and Grandfather Ward would begin about a family in a new country with two little children and a little new baby in the cradle asleep; how a great slimy snake crawled into the house, put his head over the cradle and sucked the breath and the life away from that little baby; and when the mother came in and found her little darling dead, oh, there was weeping and mourning in that house! And then we would hear of another family on the borders of a wood, with two little boys and a sister, off picking berries, and just as they had got their baskets full and were joyously starting for home, a great she wolf came out of the woods and siezed the little girl and carried her off to its den; and the little boys ran home and all they could tell their parents was that the wolf took little sister in her mouth and ran away with her, and she screaming "Ma! ma! ma!" at the top of her voice, and she was never seen or heard of more. Then grandpa would rest a little, take out his snuff-box, tap it and take a pinch; then tell us of some boys in a new country who were out at play, and played till they were tired, and then began to quarrel, fight and swear; and some bears came out of the wood and each took a boy and carried him off to their cubs, and those boys were never heard of forever. At that, the little fellow sitting next me, hunched my elbow and whispered, "same old she bears in the Sunday School lesson."

And then he would tell of emigrants in their log cabins surrounded by Indians; how they would fire and kill, and the more they killed the more would come, till ammunition would give out, and then the Indians would smash in the doors and scalp the whole family. The evening was waning, and Uncle John would come in from the mill. Louis had his mug of cider ready, and after drinking he would look into grandfather's room and say, "Oh, he's telling those same old stories for the hundredth time, and the children believe every word he says. He has told them so often that I've no doubt he believes them himself."

In those times we had a variety of holidays—the squirrel hunt, turkey shoot, ball playing, husking and apple bees, dancing parties, training and muster, and we also attended the conference and prayer meeting. Some of the deacons, like the Pharisees, invariably made long prayers, and it was safe for us boys to steal out for at least an hour, while one would remain on picket guard to warn us when to return. After the Jews and heathen were let off, he would pray that "all might redound to the glory of God." That was the signal to gather in, for the deacon was about to wind up. Our dodge game finally leaked out, and one of the fathers inquired what his boy went out for, during prayers. He said his legs got asleep sitting so long. "Go and cut me a good stout switch," said his father, "I'll wake 'em up so they won't go to sleep, I guess;" and he did.

In those days when a person had a good story to relate, he would wait for a rainy day, and then rendezvous at Uncle Ned Forbes. I frequently went, not so much for the story perhaps, as to chat with Billy and Sally. They would take me into Aunt Eunice's buttery, cut off a slice of rye and Indian bread, spread with her good butter and delicious honey, and was not that nice eating? I thought so. Then we would sit on the dye-tub—Billy and Sally on each side—and the men would range round the room eager to begin. After sending Billy down for a gallon of cider, which was soon quaffed, Mr. Carter at once told the following Vermont story: A hunter in the Green Mountains took his dogs and gun and strolled off at a season when to kill deer was forbidden by law under a heavy fine. He followed his dogs who had started a deer till he found himself in a Dutchman's yard. Calling back his dogs he peeped into the barn and found the owner dressing flax. The Dutchman had just spied the deer, and he raised his swingling knife and pointing with it exclaimed, 'Mine Gott, how I could shoot that deer if only I had my gun?" The hunter, overhearing this speech, fired himself, and the deer fell, when he rushed in and told the Dutchman he had caught him killing deer contrary to law.

Dutchy scratched his head. Said he, "Tell you what I do; you take the deer and say nothing." So the man took it over his shoulder, whistled to his dogs, slyly picked up his gun and started for home. He had not gone far when he was shouted at to stop, and coming up to him the Dutchman laid his hand on his shoulder and said: "Mr. Hunter, who would have thought the damn old swingling knife would have gone off so!"

As we grew up, we had our out-door gatherings, or as you would now say, our pic-nics. We called them then, "frolics," and we would take our girls and gather around the old grape-vine rock, and have a jolly time. There would be Pratts, Perkins, Bracketts, Wards, Forbes, Pomeroys, Putnams, Whitings, Lazelis, Grahams, Taylors, Carters, Brooks, Allens, and others, all bringing fruit from their orchards, and we would sit down and eat apples and snap the seeds at the girls, and the girls would snap the seeds at the boys and toss the cores over their shoulders to the next couple. Then came the pears, which were in every orchard in those days, and we would eat awhile on them, and the girls would snap the seeds to the boys, and the boys back again to the girls, and toss the cores over their shoulders to the next couple. Then we would have the red-cheeked old rare-ripes and white maleantoons, which luscious fruit grew beside the rocks and stones as plenty as are the bushes to-day. Of these we eat and eat till we were full. The boys tossed the stones to the girls and the girls tossed the stones back to the boys; and then we had the blue plums. Oh, those beautiful old blue plums! We eat and eat, till our teeth were set on edge. The girls tossed the stones over to the boys and the boys tossed the stones to the girls behind them. Then came the butternuts, cart-loads of them on the ground. Each boy would get a big stone and two small ones to crack with, and then with his girl on one side and himself on the other, they would crack and eat, and eat and crack jokes, and when the young beau could get a meat whole, they would blush and divide. So we cracked and eat and threw the shucks over our shoulders to the next pair; and with walnuts we would do the same, always looking out to give as much as was sent. When we were thirsty, there was the old, cold spring down in the dell below the rock. How many times have I been down on all-fours to drink at that cold, sparkling spring, but when we were going in genteel couples, Aunt Eunice had Sally wash up the small gourd and give Billy to carry to frolic, and Aunt Ruth would tell Emmons to take the piggin, not the large one in the shed but the little one by the spring, so we had the piggin and the gourd. By pairs we went down to the cold spring, and the boys dipped the gourd and handed it to the girl, and dipped the piggin and they drank; then the girl handed the boy the gourd and the boy handed the girl the piggin; so they both drank out of the piggin and the gourd, and handed it to the next pair waiting. O, who ever drank anything that tasted so good as that water at the old spring out of the gourd and the piggin—unless it may be to put your forehead under the iron bail of the old oaken bucket with the chimb poised on the edge of the well-curb, and this is about the same thing! And then we would scatter off in groups and pairs among the wild grape-vines, and when the day waned and we all met together again, to go home, lo! on the cheeks of the girls were many purple stains, and no wonder; for the boys had eaten so heartily of the grapes. It was no trouble to make ready for home, nothing to pick up but the gourd and the piggin, neither had we been to any expense for railroad fare, nor did father meet us with a scowl that the wagon was broken, the whip lost, and he was afraid old Dobbin was foundered. No! it had cost us nothing to go on foot, and our caterer at the pic-nic had been the cook of Nature, and we eat freely of her abundance and were satisfied, and had no occasion to find fault. O, those were pleasant excursions, full of youthful merriment and fun, and who will say they did not yield more solid enjoyment than the higher priced ones of to-day?

There was a good deal of courting here in those times, but I cannot speak much from experience, as I was not out of my teens when I left the town. I will acknowledge that two pretty lasses showed the proverbial shrewdness of the Buckland girls by giving me the mitten—flat. Did I feel bad? Oh yes, some bad; but in our teens we are apt to get over these feelings about as soon as home-sickness, when we come in sight of the old home.

One afternoon when my mother had for company Mrs. Pomeroy, Mrs. Pratt, Aunt Sophia and Widow Trowbridge—all godly women of godly families—I sat in the door-way whistling and whittling, and hearing them talk of the church and town matters, and of their own families and children; also of their daughters, and Mrs. Trowbridge spoke of her godly son. That evening as father and mother were talking over the visit, it was suggested that the godly son and one of Mrs. Pomeroy's daughters would make a good match. Soon after at some public meeting at Ashfield, behold, the godly son and his sister and Miss Pomeroy drive up! I stop here; if you wish to know further ask my old friend there, Mr. Silas Trowbridge.

But I must tell you of one of those old weddings from the homestead of Deacon Torrey, who lived across the river in Granny McNutt's hollow. The bridegroom was Tommy Carter, son of old Grandfather Elias Carter, and a spruce little fellow he was, somewhat haughty, and proud of his horsemanship, though he always rode with his legs stretched straight out. His horse was well groomed, and his saddle, bridle and spurs all toady; and with his mother's pillion covered with red velvet for his girl to sit behind him, he cut a very gay appearance. The day of the wedding had come. Mr. Spaulding had tied the knot; the bowl and the cake had been passed around, and the groomed horses had been mounted. A saddle and pillion with the young man and his mate was what equipped each horse, and ten of these with ten gay couples made up the cavalcade. They swept down by Mr. Putnam's and Mr. May's, and across the John Ward mill bridge, and Uncle John shut down the gate, looked at Tommy, hitched up his breeches but said nothing, for Tommy's father brought good grists to his mill. They went on till they passed Dr. Holbrook's, where

Abijah Thayer now lives, and were nearing the Brooks' blacksmith shop, when an unearthly yell met their ears which resounded from hill to hilltop. At the shop was Tommy's cousin John Carter, who had not been invited to the wedding; so he had got a lever about thirty feet long, and stationed himself and Kilborn ready to pry, and was screaming at the top of his voice for them to "stop! *Soon they would pry the shop out of the way so they could pass!*"

Deacon Tobey had another fair daughter, who married Mr. Ephraim Williams, and I can almost hear his shrill voice and loud laugh mingled with that of Calvin Nelson, as they were laying wall. Mr. Williams always said he would raise a girl for *me*, but the girl never came to time. I believe, however, he filled the bill for my friend, Abijah Thayer.

In every history of Buckland, writers have uniformly spoken well of her schools, and from the earliest times her citizens seem to have paid earnest attention to the education of their children, and fitting them for the duties and struggles of life. Their summer schools, in my early days, were taught by the Misses White, of Heath, and the winter terms by Mr. Erastus Taylor, Mr. Shepard, Mr. Tobey and Mr. Porter. Later than this, you know as well as I, and still later, you had teachers of your own sons and daughters, whom you know better than I do. I should also mention a class of about twenty young men who were taught arithmetic, by Uncle Ned Forbes, at his own house. The earliest select school in my memory was taught by Mr. Daniel Forbes, of Furbush, who was called by the boys "little holy Daniel." He was a teacher by nature, mild and pleasant; I never saw a scholar out of place, nor saw him use the ferrule or switch; while in Mr. Tobey's school, I have the most lively recollection of both. Mr. Forbes kept school in both of my father's shops, and in his upper hall, also at Mr. Benjamin Carter's, and I think in the large shed room of Jabez Brooks. He also taught in the west, south and east part of town, but perhaps those were exclusively writing schools. He wrote a beautiful, round hand, and in it made out many of the family records in those days,—oftentimes adding beneath a suitable verse. I have seen Miss Mary Lyon sit behind one of the work benches in my father's shop, and write and study under his instruction. She also wrote that fine, old fashioned round hand, acquired through his copy. O, I revere the memory of Mr. Forbes and Mr. Porter! They did more to lift the young men from ignorance to information than any others I ever knew.

Who remembers the old spelling schools in Buckland, when we collected from the north and the south, and the east and the west, and were called up and spelled down, and jolly good times we had, both with the spelling and going home with the girls. Is it not so? And then our debating schools, which the *fathers* attended, for a little fun; how well I remember them all, and, particularly the first in which I myself took a part, not yet in my teens. Late in the evening I was called upon, when I returned that I thought the question had already been fully disgusted. This raised a titter, and Mr. Porter sprang to his feet, said the boy was

3

not far out of the way, for the question *had* been very poorly handled. Mr. Porter would always come to the assistance of the boys in a *school,* but as a church tithing-man, we had a terrible dread of him. I have seen him take a boy by the ears, and with his legs dangling carry him half way across the meeting house, and sit him down behind him, *hard,* in the singer-seats. Uncle Levi Taylor, the shoemaker, was also a tithing man, and he never looked so pleasant to me on Sunday as he did when I was sitting long evenings in his shop in my stocking feet, having my boots mended. He tooted out of the same tooter that Mr. Porter did to pitch the tune, and wore the same linsey vest the first time I ever saw him and the last. The last debating school I attended was at the Four Corners, and I remember well the leading disputants—Calvin Pomeroy and Andrew Butler, on the question, which was the least risk, to lend money on interest, or invest it in farming or trade? Mr. Pomeroy, who was keen and full of fun, turned on Andrew, who had never had much experience in lending money, and, said he, "did you ever in your life time lose a cent of interest?" "Yes," replied Adrew, "I have lost a good deal, and I am now losing more than a thousand dollars every year for the want of the principal to draw it." According to Mr. Butler's logic, are we not all sustaining heavy losses to-day?

Who does not remember the old speaking school kept by Mr. Porter, usually at the Mill Yard? Over from Charlemont came the Averys, the Ballards, the Maxwells and others to join us. These schools did much to develope the young men and help to overcome their bashfulness, and Mr. Porter is mainly entitled to the credit of it. I would not be afraid to ask my old friend, Silas Trobridge, to-day, if those schools did not do a great deal to bring diffident boys, like him and myself, out of this diffidence into public speakers.

We had at one time what was called the "mad dog scare." A boy went to Jabez Brooks' shop to have his horse shod, seeing a dog lying on the floor, roused him with a stick, whereupon he ran out of the barn. Afterwards Mrs. Brooks discovered the dog with glaring eyes and frothing mouth lying in front of the cow. By means of a pitchfork she kept him at bay as he snapped at her, while she ran to the shop to notify Mr. Brooks. Kilborn jumped upon the horse, half shod, and took down the old long gun, that was always loaded and hanging upon the brackets, with powder horn and pouch full; the dog ran toward the Mill Yard, snapping at every thing he passed, and Kilborn followed, punching his heels into the horse and yelling at the top of his voice: "*Look out for the mad dog.*" Passing the Mill Yard, Charles White was bringing out a grist for a boy on horseback. He dropped the grist, and catching the gun from the wall, mounted the horse, and it being fresh, he was soon neck and nought with Kilborn. They ran, and the dog ran, but the men pushed so closely that at the Thayer road the dog turned up; the riders just twitched the reins and dropped back, brought up the old guns, fired, and the dog fell dead. The cow was put in the pound behind the sheds and was soon running mad, as was evident from her red eyes and shaking head, tongue hanging out of her mouth, and keeping up an unearthly bellowing. Mr. Brooks, Samuel Taylor and Mr. Bachelor came with a rope that they used to draw in oxen to be shod, got on top of the pound, made a noose in the middle of the rope, dropped it on to her horns, and opened the gate. Mr. Taylor was at one end and Mr. Bachelor at the other to keep her at bay. Mr. Brooks following with gun, and Kilborn with ax and shovel, and the boys on behind. Down the hill and about half way to the Batcheler bridge, the grave was waiting. Mr. Brooks fired and she dropped dead in the grave. The rope was thrown in, the grave was filled up, and that was the end of the mad dog scare. Years after, a freshet washed out the skeleton of that cow, but in my day I never knew a boy with courage enough to touch one of those bones.

Many of you remember the bitter and exciting lawsuit with Conway about the Reniff family—three years in court and then left to reference and lost. I remember, as yesterday, when Mr. Chapin, the agent, came back,—we were building the Graham house and all stopped to hear the story. There was loud talk and some swearing about how Buckland had been tricked and wronged; but the first thing was to raise the money—$350—and settle before additional cost of judgment. Right then and there a note was made out to the Northampton bank. Esquire Chápin and Major Griswold signed it with Sir Brooks for surety. Mr Brooks required the Selectmen to give him a note to secure him against loss. Here are the two notes and they appear to be paid. But calamities never come single-handed. Mrs. Reniff increased the population and also the paupers two in one night. Then there was another storm, and how Dr.Allen ipped and scolded that "she ought to know better; it was outrageous for paupers—two at a time!" This raised her dander, and she retorted: "Don't you see I have the worst of it, and don't you know twins can't be had for the asking, or stopped for the wishing?" Well, in those days when the paupers were getting too plenty, the citizens clubbed together, got two yoke of oxen, Mr. Trowbridge's great ox wagon covered with tow cloth, packed in Jim McNutt and his family, and started them west to grow up with the country. Brigham Carter took the whip, and was ordered not to give it up till they were beyond North river. Jim was the only man I ever knew that could put a quart of cider into his stomach without swallowing. Long years after, in passing through Buckland,who should I meet but Jim McNutt! Said he had prospered, "raised fourteen hundred bushels of wheat last year, built a good barn this season, and daughter Roba was well married, with children as plenty as her mother's." Would it not be well to send more Jim McNutts to grow up with the country?

Who does not remember Uncle Zenas Graham with his pleasant face, who was always ready to buy the sheep skin when you had the wool pulled off, and give you 12½ cents for it, and 25 cents for every deacon-skin. Mr. Graham tanned good leather, and so did Mr. Townsley after him, and Mr. Caswell after him. I know, for I bought it for belting. But don't you remember those nice velvet-soft deacon-skins that Uncle Zenas and Uncle Nuel used to dress? These were made into slippers for the girls to dance in, and were always bought for the wedding shoes. Uncle Nuel once had an extra nice one finished, and called me in to ask if I "didn't think that deacon-skin would make shoes good enough for one of Aunt Sophy's girls." "Yes," I told him, "or for any other girl." I do not know positively, but am of opinion that Aunt Mit stepped up to be married in that same deacon-skin. Now I want to digress here to say that I know of no possible connection or comparison between the first officer in the church and a young calf's hide. If your Committee can explain why I was selected to deliver this address over the shoulders of a hundred more competent, they may be able to solve this riddle; but I confess they are both inexplicable to me, and I am particular to say so, for I do not want your children's children at your next Centennial, to come and rap on my mossy grave-stone to enquire if it is a *fact*, that in my time the deacons were killed and skinned, and their hides tanned to make slippers and wedding shoes.

I come now to Miss Mary Lyon, who surpassed all the female teachers we ever had in Buckland. She rose from a lowly origin, spent her younger years in family industries, spinning and weaving like other girls of those times. I have often seen her, horseback, carrying her cloth to Mr. Pomeroy's to be dressed, and her reeds to Fobes to be repaired. She was a rosy, robust-looking girl, and spent most of the time in her youth at the old homestead, which you must well remember. Much of her early schooling she received at the corner near Mr. Clark's—sometimes coming from home two miles, and sometimes boarding at Uncle Spencer Woodward's, doing chores for her board. Mr. Porter mostly kept these schools, and procured for Mary her first situations to teach. She first kept in what was called Thayer district, in 1814, and at the close of the term there was some disappointment at the lack of progress, and Mr. Porter hired her again in 1815 to keep the same school, and her friends were happily disappointed to see the progress made both by herself and her scholars. In 1816 she kept the Centre school. My father was then making the brick for his house, and she would often come up to the yard and say to me that she wanted to learn to make brick, and would help me turn them up and put them on the wheel-barrow, and afterwards on the hakes. Who can tell what was in her mind, and if she had not, even then, a glimmering of the great future for which Providence was fitting her. She taught a school I think, at Baptist Corner from 1817 to 19, and in Alpheus Brooks' house, when she went to Byfield. I next met her at Ashfield academy in 1821, where she was both teaching and studying. In 1824 she opened the first of her select schools in Buckland. Two of them were kept in my father's hall, and two in Mr. Graham's; and I challenge you to-day to point me out any schools in Western Franklin that equal them in intelligence and progress. After she had kept two seasons in my father's hall, the Ashfield people beset her to come back there, which she agreed to do if she could have a suitable place in which to teach. J. Lilly, Mr. Pratt and myself were employed to turn the old academy building back and put a hall in the top of it, which made a very good room. Here she kept two winters, when Ashfield insisted that she must also remain summers, as it almost vacated the academy while she was away with Mrs. Grant. Then Buckland stepped in and offered a chance, and as father's hall was high up and not large enough, it was agreed to fit up a new place, and all the old joiners chipped in and Graham's hall was built about as quick as Jonah's gourd grew. Here she kept two schools, and, in the meantime, a plan was maturing to make a permanent school here by buying the place now occupied by Dr. Trow and extending to the Griswold line, and also to take in the then White Jones place. The funds were forthcoming; but whether it was her foresight or the direction of Providence, the location was placed in a more suitable place. I would like to review the life of Mary Lyon as written by Miss White, but first let me state the facts. Mr. Ferry, who married this Miss White, first courted Mary Lyon, and expected to marry her and she fully expected to marry him: but Mrs. White, a keen, thin-faced, long-nosed woman, persuaded him that her daughter Amanda would be more suitable for the wife of a missionary to Mackinaw, and he left Mary and took Amanda. It was a Providential change, for Amanda made a good missionary, and Miss Lyon greatly excelled in the field she herself occupied. But Miss White's book says "she sold her linen, being in straitened circumstances, to get the means to continue her studies." Now Miss Lyon never was in reduced straits, nor did you ever see one of the name that was. She sold her accumulations because she saw the uncertainties of man's promises, and she then and there decided to devote her life to the great cause of education, and to her God who never deceived or forsook her. The book also undertakes to prove that she was a slattern—for you can't make much less of it. Now I knew Mary Lyon from a girl down to near the close of her life, and I never saw her when she was not dressed neat and tidy, and good enough for the position which she occupied. I also knew Ashfield Plain well. The Paines and Whites were aristocratic families with whom I lived for two years. They treated me well, and I have no quarrel with them to-day; but when I first went to Ashfield they sneered at me on account of my dress. I wore the home-made suit my mother had spun and wove in her house. Mr. Pomeroy had dressed the cloth, and Aunt Patty Whiting made it up,—and I wore it out, too, in spite of the jeers about the pepper and salt suit; and I will add that after I had been there two years, digging away with all my inferior talent, I did not have to go to the brothers and sisters of this historian to find out how to analyse an intricate Latin phrase, or to work a hard problem in mathematics. This book also claims that her tuition was given her at the academy, but the truth was that she heard recitations enough to more than balance her tuition. Miss Lyon was a Buckland woman, and her attachments were here until she gathered up all for her Hadley home; and so long as Clesson's river runs seaward, and her borders are surrounded by the old Buckland homes, so long among these hills will linger the fragrance of her memory.

We now come to the merchants, ministers and physicians of Buckland —thankful to say we had no lawyers. Our tradesmen were Brooks, Jones, Hubbard, Maj. Tyler, Capt. Mayhew, Lazell, Hitchcock, Wells, Ward, Maynard and Ballard, and since their time I am unacquainted. They went to market twice a year and all that we had then was fresh and new. Now-a-days if we do not replenish every other day from the drummer, our goods are called counter-worn. Well, these men supplied the families with dry goods and groceries, and if wives and daughters did not have the variety they do to-day? it was just as well—they never missed it. Dress-making did not cost what it does now, but when we grumble at our bills, let us remember that the sewing-girl is perhaps like Aunt Delia Thayer, keeping father and mother or aunt away from public charity; and if her filial devotion does not merit reward, what can we expect? In the way of trade we had one corn speculator that I must not omit to mention. While my father's brick house was building, and the workmen slept in the garret of the great shop, in the dead of the night we heard a fearful scream. All got up and hurried out, David Taylor on ahead. When we reached the meeting house we could hear the distant cry of "murder." On we went, till at the bridge over Taylor's brook, we found Stephen Nelson on his back at the bottom of the brook, ten bushels of corn on top of him, and his horse and wagon on top of the corn. We extricated him from his difficulty, found him uninjured and it leaked out that Uncle Stephen had heard that corn was eighty cents a bushel a few miles below the Falls, and only seventy cents at the Falls, so he was going to make a dollar by a speculation. Perhaps you may think a dollar was a small margin, but I tell you a dollar in those days looked as big as a cart wheel does now. Mr. Hubbard always blackguarded Mr. Nelson about his corn speculation, and he never heard the last of it. For a generation or more I have been acquainted with that great speculating Wall street in New York, and have seen multitudes with their pockets full of rocks, go in and take a flyer. Some few have become millionaires, but most of them have returned penniless, cursing the ingratitude, the cheat, deception and wrong practiced upon them; but who cares for their wail? In the light of to-day I look upon Mr. Nelson as a successful speculator. He took ten bushels of corn and went out to speculate, and, with all its hazards, he returned at night with the same amount increased in bulk, like most speculations, by being watered.

With the exception of Dr. Holbrook, who passed away before my day, the medical men of Buckland were all known to me. He, with Drs. Allen, Long, Axtell and brothers Trow, constitute the whole from the settlement of the town. Of old Dr. Allen only will I speak. He was a waspy old fellow, hated boys, and would swear at them like a piper in his younger days. Many a time has he threatened to sieze me by the nose and dose me with jalap and calomel. I suppose the modern M. D. would weaken this a little and call it "salts and senna," but so far as the taste and smell are concerned it would be about the same thing. If a person was ailing in those days and called in the doctor, no matter what the difficulty was, the main practice was to stick the lancet into him the first thing and draw off what little vitality he had. Often have I seen persons faint holding the dish for blood, but *I* never fainted, and used to think as a prejudiced boy that I could hold the dish calmly if the old doctor's jugular vein had been tapped. One Saturday night he was called to see Roswell Butler, who had been well and at singing-school the night before. As usual he stuck in his lancet, not knowing what ailed him, but coming up early the next morning found he had the spotted fever, and exclaimed at once, " I swear, Roswell, I've killed you!" and before nine o'clock he was a corpse. When the matter was first agitated of putting a stove in the meeting house the doctor opposed it bitterly; would rather they should keep up a fire on the common for the boys and girls to toast their shins Sunday noons: but the stove was put in. Later in life he became a professed christian and used to say he was educating his only son for a minister and hoped the Lord would prepare his heart. Joseph built better than his father thought: he turned out a fair farmer. On the whole let us speak well of Dr. Allen. He had his faults and his good qualities, toiled for the sick to the last and dropped in his harness. Peace to his ashes in the old burying ground! Of the doctor's wife, Mrs. Allen, I will say that her train when she first came to Buckland was even longer than the ladies have them at the present day, and required the services of a negro boy to carry it handsomely behind her.

The first church society in Buckland dates with the settlement of the town, and Mr. Josiah Spaulding, who was settled between 1780-90, was the first permanent minister. I knew him perfectly well and worked for him a great deal. A noble old man he was. I have in my day heard many of the noted preachers of this country, but none of them have inspired me with the respect I have for the memory of old Mr. Spaulding. His oddities no man could number, and I must mention a few. It is related of him that being at Ashfield at an association he hitched his horse at the end of the shed by the bars, and when he came to go home he found his bridle run through two post holes, and some other wrinkles which he did not understand. Mr. S. looked and looked; and said " the horse had undoubtedly gone through the post-holes, but he didn't think he could get him back and so he would have to cut the bridle." The boys were doubtless mischievous, but I will vouch that three of those boys made good Congregational ministers. Once when they were laying wall up that steep hill between Mr. Pratt and himself, and they were lifting one end of a heavy stone and Mr. Hall the other, Mr. Hall, who you know was a very profane man, sang out, " Damn you! why don't you lift?" Mr. Spaulding let go, saying, "Oh, you mustn't swear!" and down went the stone to the bottom of the hill. On the Carter & Negress place was a great quantity of peaches, which somehow or other the boys would get. Mr. Spaulding said he "did not care so much about the peaches, but it was wrong to leave so much temptation for the boys to steal;" so he picked and carried them up to Israel Williams' and had them distilled into brandy, about ten gallons. Now here is a question for your debating society, " Which is the greater wrong, to steal peaches or drink the brandy?" Mr. Spaulding was very liberal with his pulpit. Elder Ward, brother to John, used to come around occasionally and Mr. S. would let him have the use of it for half a day. Mr. Ward was one of the noisy kind, and pounded away hard on the pulpit, and I always kept my eye close on the man's hand that held up the sounding-board, expecting every moment he would scare him so as to let it fall, but he held on faithfully for about seventy years, when I suppose modern philanthropy relieved him. The town records being destroyed, we can never know with certainty, but we should like to be informed whether this sounding-board man was retired on a pension or was cast aside as having outlived his usefulness. All the old people must remember the great revival called the Clary revival, because Mr. Clary of Conway was engaged in it for a long time. Everything was at a fever heat, a great many inquiring and many more shouting Hosanna. The meetings in all parts of the town were held to a late hour at night and again at an early hour in the morning. Business was greatly suspended and land left untilled. Mr. Spaulding was getting old and declined to attend these extra meetings. He was a cool old gentleman and carried a level head in many things and it was a bomb-shell thrown in that heated community when he remarked in his pulpit that "these too-numerous and late nightly gatherings were not in keeping with the public good or the best morals of the people." After sixty years of reflection I am inclined to think Mr. Spaulding was right and we young folks wrong. O, that we could go back to the halcyon days of Mr. Spaulding! You would see Moses Nelson come to meeting with his oxen, bringing his mother and sisters, and Mr. Ned Forbes go in at the front door with his leather apron on and turn to the left to his pew; all the congregation plainly dressed—myself barefoot at fifteen years of age, for those were the days when families were reared in industry, frugality and simplicity. Mr. Spaulding was sorely afflicted in the calamity which befel his only son. The long years of naked idiotcy in his wooden cage are familiar to you all. The care and attention he received were all and more than could be expected, for when a human being is bereft of reason he sinks immeasurably below the brute. In nothing perhaps do the times show more intelligent advance than in the understanding and treatment of the insane.

Of the Baptist society the record says: "a feeble church about half a century ago and finally died out." This record may seem correct but it gives a wrong impression. The fact is that among the earliest settlers of this town was a large number of Baptist people, the Putnams, Mays, Lackeys, Forbes, Batchelors, Taylors, Whitings, Lyons and many more; but the church building happened to be over the line in Ashfield, as yonder church is now in Shelburne; but stand with me on that long iron bridge of a Sunday and see how many cross over to that brick church from this Buckland side. Just so in those times. The Baptists were here as numerous as the others, and they helped build up this town and rear those large families from the first settlement.

So of the Methodists. The record says, "no public place of worship till about fifty years from the incorporation of the town." The record is correct, yet the facts are these: In early times the Methodists did not believe in meeting houses. They were a people of great plainness and simplicity and preferred to hold their meetings in barns and sheds, in the public highway, or in the forest about Catamount den; they met as they did in apostolic days wherever they could collect a crowd, no matter if it was simply under the canopy of heaven. But they have changed and now conform more to the general customs of other societies. The women became tired of sitting all day in a partly-cleaned stable, with their boys dangling their limbs over the high beams overhead, as I have many times seen them. Well, the Baptists have modified that nasal twang so peculiar to them seventy years ago, and the Methodists have lowered the tone in which Elder Ward spoke when I was worried about the sounding-board. So all have had their modifications, and to-day you cannot tell a Methodist or Baptist from the old order; and the old order, though backed up by the whole power of the State until recently, has been greatly modified and changed. Our old Methodists were Father Rawson, one of the sixty to storm Stony Point, the Davises, the Peltons, some of the Wards, all the Woods, Forbses, some of the Tobys and Bracketts, the Perkins, the Woodwards, the Clarks, the Mallories, the Spragues and the Johnsons, and others whom I do not now think of,—these all have contributed to the building up and support of this town, and their descendants are scattered far and wide over our populous country. Of children, I believe Josiah Johnson scored 20, against Uncle Brooks 17, the next highest, and from that number down to a baker's dozen the families were numerous. Your Speaker, not having very high aspirations in building up a community, has rested where his own father and Samuel Taylor, 2d, rested, and was satisfied by scoring a baker's dozen.

Of Shelburne Falls it becomes me to say a very little. When I left Buckland the two Coleman farms and Lieut. Ellis' constituted the village of Shelburne Falls on the Buckland side. Mr. Nims' in the bend,—Mr. Eddy's, Mr. White's and Mr. Field's, the two Thayers' and Fullers', and all the land behind. The bridge was built about ten years before I left. It was a Burr bridge and built by Mr. Sheldon of Deerfield, Capt. Johnson doing the stone work. Mr. Ellis was the main man that pushed the project through. Scott's bridge was built by Consider Scott about ten years later, under contract, by which he lost considerable money. Allen Barnard did the wood work and Capt. Johnson the masonry. About the last of my work in Buckland was to help build this bridge. Before the time of these bridges we used to ford the river at Taylor's in Charlemont, and, if the water was low, cross and come by the Hotchkiss place, and if extremely low, have crossed just above the bridge, but it was not safe. I once undertook it here when the water was higher than I had expected, and my horse and wagon had to swim. I stepped on the king bolt to keep it in, and got out safely, but received a reprimand from my mother for wetting the grist. When the water was very high we went by Ashfield, Conway and Deerfield to Greenfield. Every little while came up the ringing cry that somebody had gone over the Falls, and once I recollect of going a long way down below the Falls where a decayed body had been found. The services were held on the spot and the body buried in the sand. Since I left Buckland you have built up a beautiful village, and have factories and workshops that are a credit to the builders and the town. You have industrious mechanics and intelligent merchants. You have supported excellent schools and raised your own teachers. This is well. I have recently looked over the old ledgers of several towns, and what do I find? Toddy, toddy, toddy, flip, flip, flip, rum, brandy and sugar for ministers and all. Perhaps the seller made money, but it often made him a drunkard, and his sons, too. Now, your fine equipages, your horses and carriages, your nice houses and furniture are all legitimate outlays, and mark the advanced stage of civilization and refinement. The laborer gets every dollar you spend, and there is nothing any plainer in the arrangements of Providence than that he who has more talent must lay out work for him that has less. The trouble is not that you spend, but your idleness. When the low descending sun goes down on your misspent day, all the power that you possess, and all that your Maker has given you, cannot recall the misspent day. It is lost—forever lost, to you, to the world, and to your God.

At the close of the address there was an intermission for dinner. S. A. Little, of Shelburne Falls had a large tent erected in the adjacent lot, where plates were laid for five or six hundred people. A good dinner was furnished, but the caterer was not overcrowded with patrons. The frugal people chose to rely upon their lunch baskets rather than the public "spread," and gathered in little knots and family groups about the grove and picnicked after the old fashion. It was a very pretty scene. The clouds, which for a time had overcast the sky, were dispelled, and everybody was put in his holiday humor. Old people got together and talked over "Auld Lang Syne;" "city cousins" had a taste of genuine rural enjoyment, and in the outskirts of the grove lovers walked and talked, quite as oblivious of the outside world as were their grandparents in the days of Mr. Griswold's gourd and piggin. A. L. Ward, a Fall River pohtographer, a native of Buckland, by the way, improved the occasion to take pictures of a group, composed of the Centennial Committee of Arrangements, the orator and officers of the day. He made two negatives—one for a stereoscopic view and the other a larger picture suitable for framing—and was quite successful in his work.

In the afternoon the people reassembled at the speaker's stand for another feast of good things. Hon. Henry Winn was the master of ceremonies, and first introduced Mrs. Ella C. Drabble, who read the following poem:

## Mrs. Drabbles's Poem.

Sweet gift of song to most denied
  And richly given to few,
Upon those lips, devoid of grace,
  Descend like twilight dew.
Some worthier hand should lift the lyre
  And sound your glorious themes,—
Lips that are touched by heavenly fire,
  Breathe music sweet as dreams!
Would, Buckland, that to-day for thee
  Some rock of song was riven,
And words, like streams of water, free,
  Forth from its heart were given.
O, then in notes of purest sound
  Thy grace and worth we'd sing,
While the hills our peaceful vale surround,
  With echoes glad should ring.

    But take each line,
      Each faltering line,
O, waiting hearts, and call them thine;—
    Supply their dearth,
    And make them worth
The joyful day that gives them birth.

Dear Buckland, round thy name we twine
Thine own staunch oak and feathery pine:
With willing feet we gather here,
    Our hearts elate,
    To celebrate
Thy happy hundredth year!

Thy sons and daughters at thy call,
Have left their pleasure and their toil;
Their welcome be our glad refrain
Till breeze and stream repeat the strain.
Our mother bids them welcome home,
As to these old time scenes they come;
She folds us all within her arms,
Unveils for us her sweetest charms.
Dear are her forests old and grand,
Her hills that rise on every hand,
Her rocky pastures, meadows fair,
Brooks that with music fill the air.
Dear are her churches,—in their walls
What sacred scenes to-day recalls;
What happy brides have trod their aisles,
When earth to them was wreathed in smiles!
Oft did the man of sorrows meet
Within their gate the mourners' feet;
What words of comfort and of grace
Still echo from each holy place!
Dear are her schools, for round them twine
Bright hopes that on our future shine;
These nurseries call for fondest care,
Our heartiest aid, our tenderest care:
Their power for good or ill, how great!
For in them lies the nation's fate.
Dear are her graveyards, quaint and old,
Where honored forms have turned to mold:
Root out the nettle and the thorn,—
With rarest flowers those graves adorn.
Shame on the town, whate'er her name,
That unfulfilled leaves the claim,
The sad, sweet claim the dead may ask!
Say, shall our hands refuse the task?
O, brightly let God's acre bloom,
And roses crown the darkest tomb.

All peacefully the years glide by
  Within our quiet vale.
The record of our early days
  Lives but as an evening tale
We tell to the children by the fire
  When blows the wintry gale.

Think not, because our lives are calm,
  They flow in sluggish round;
Yon stream is deep, its waters pass
  With scarce a murmuring sound.
No life so narrow but its love

Some other life hath crowned.
Brave hearts within our midst have beat,
  Great souls have here been born;
And some have wandered far from where
  They passed life's dewey morn;
Their gifts a wider range have sought,
  And larger fields adorn.

A gnarled old tree, a broken wall,
  Are all that mark the place
Where first the daylight softly fell
  On Mary Lyon's face.
So like a star that name hath shone
  That none hath failed to trace.

Embalm their names with memory's dew,
And bare the head with reverence true
In honor of the hardy few
Whose strokes resounded through and
    through
The wooded hill, the silent glade,
As first their lonely homes they made.
Those names alone make Buckland strong.—
In hearts they live, uncarved on stone;
She matches them in deeds of worth,
The honest life, the tranquil hearth;
And if her faults are plain to name,
Shall children speak a mother's blame?
How freely in her country's need
Has Buckland bid her sons God-speed;
Thrice hath she given her young, her brave,
The Nation's honor fair to save.

Say not that love has made us blind;
That is not love of truest kind
Whose eyes are blinded by the power
Of passions for a fleeting hour.
The highest love doth never pass
Unnoticed faults of any class;
But seeing all, loves on, forgiving:—
'Tis this which makes life worth the living.

A sigh for the past, the good old days
  Of simple joys and healthful ways,
With little to blame, and much to praise;
  Much we with pride recall.

Our feet may tread a wider plain,
But many a weary heart would fain
Take up the simple faith again
  In which our fathers died.

Their happy spirits downward glance
To-day, and all our joy enhance;
And if they smile on us, perchance
  Our hearts shall catch the thrill.

A song for the present,—a song of praise
As clear and fresh as a morning breeze
When it whispers through the budding trees
  In the sunny month of May.

O, happy homes! that nestle snug
  In Buckland's pleasant nooks!
O, happy children, born beside
  Her rippling, babbling brooks!

Blest are the hearts that in such homes
Have found their joy and rest;
Thrice blest the souls that win from life
  The truest and the best.

The homes and hearts are ours,
  To shape the future as we will,
And dark or fair the dawning years
  As we our niches fill.

A wish for her future, O, brighter by far
Than light of the moon or vesper star,
Brighter than sunset's radiant hue,
Or the glittering drops of early dew,
Brighter than flowers in dark, drear days,
Or pearly snow in the sunlight's rays,
That round her name like starry wreath

May glow the honors years bequeath,
That all her coming days shall be
Marked by a true prosperity,
That hope and joy for her shall sing,
And peace brood soft with folded wing,
Diviner life her churches show,
And more of heaven on earth bestow,
A charity on them descend
That shall new grace their dealings lend.
Their ways reveal (they have not yet)
More love of God than love of sect.
Our strongest hope that we may be
A nation strong, and clean and free
Lies in our schools; withhold no more
The aid that shall augment their power,
Nor think an effort vainly made
That moves them towards a higher grade.
Book lore alone is small, indeed;
But free from party sect or creed,
Their future shall be rich, and they
shall rise to hights unknown to-day.

O, that the rich within the gate
Might freely want and care abate,
The poor no more in envy pine
Because his friend drinks fortune's wine,
Nor we in selfishness, alone
Look on the things that are our own,
No drunkard on our streets be found,
Our Sabbaths broken by no sound
That on the restful air shall jar,
But peace and order everywhere.
Make haste, O, gracious days, make haste;
Thy fruits though we may never taste,
This fervent wish our hearts shall hold
Until in death these hearts are cold;
Although our eyes may fail to see
That the blest time shall surely be
When of the living, or o'er the dead
More faithful praise cannot be said,
No words of higher, just renown
Than this: "He lived in Buckland town."

Next came letters from absent Buckland sons who found it impossible to respond in person to the Committee's invitation. The writers were Judson S. Brown, in one of the departments at Washington, Rev. Lathrop Taylor, President of Wheaton College, of Wheaton, Illinois, and Hon. Bushnell White, U. S. Marshal at Cleveland, Ohio.

## Mr. White's Letter.

CLEVELAND, June 6, 1879.

*Frederick Forbes, Esq., Dear Sir:* Your favor of June 4th is just received. It would give me the greatest pleasure to be present, could I command my own time, but my business and other arrangements for the summer and early fall will, necessarily, prevent my attendance. I hope you will persevere in your efforts, for I am sure you will have good times. The old town and its former inhabitants have never been forgotten. Every foot of ground from the Falls and Deerfield river to Ashfield and Hawley are as familiar now as they were fifty years ago. I can recall every house on the old road from the Falls to Ward's saw-mill south of the Center, and each face looking out from them, as clearly as an event of yesterday. First, came Uncle Oliver Coleman, then Lieutenant Ellis, next Sam Ellis, who married Aunt "Nabby Johnson, my school teacher, when a small, bare-footed boy of six; and those same feet yet tingle at the recollection of her tall, spare figure, and the switch never out of her hand; how I wished for boots in those days. Now we pass Eddy's, and ascending somewhat, leave Capt. Zebulon White on the left, with whom lives his son-in-law, Field; down the hill, across the pine woods brook, we come where my grandfather Thompson lived and died. A few rods farther, going up a small hill, you will still see, I think on the left, a stone wall fence, laid up by my father and I in 1829. Fingers and back ache at the thought. Now we pass Little brook and Clesson's river, and arrive at the mill-yard. Father's house, saw and grist mill on the left, Josiah Thompson's, Major Taylor's and Barney Wells' on the right; next comes my old friend Silas Trowbridge. Does he still live? Now comes the stay, the defence, the pride of Massachusetts, a school-house, the old brick school-house of the north district. I love and revere it still. Bound fast in its recollections is the fragrant memory of John Porter, the *best* teacher I have ever seen. We have famous teachers and famous schools in this city, but none of the former equalled Deacon John in his method of teaching, in the interest excited, and in the results accomplished. He taught in that house in winters of 1826-27-28. He was a good and great man; lieutenant and captain of the artillery, the best drilled company in the county or state; superintendent of the Sunday-school and leader of the church choir. The first thing that attracted my childish notion in church, was the sounding board just ready to fall on the gray head of good old Parson Spaulding: the second astonishing thing was the tuning fork of Deacon Porter. He will not need it upon the "other side." His goodness and honesty, his love and labor for his fellow-men will rightly pitch his voice to the melody of heaven. Passing from this, to me, dear spot, I come to Levi Taylor's, then to Enos Taylor's, and following the road around the curve of the river, we find another bridge across the Clesson's river. There is no dwelling on the side-hill upon the right, for Gardner Wilder was a school-boy then, and lived with his father, Captain Wilder, forty rods further on, on the left of the road. Next, we pass Nathaniel Wilder's; over another bridge we come to the poor house. Just beyond this, leaving the river road, and turning to the right we cross a small brook, and commence creeping up the hill, (as hard to climb as the ascent to Heaven by the Orthodox road) and find the old church in the angle formed by two long rows of horse sheds. Horse sheds! for our fathers were kinder to their animals than they believed God could be to man. Indeed, fear of that " hot place," or something else, made them refuse for years to have a fire in church, even in the coldest weather. Perhaps it was too suggestive of the possible outcome in the next world. Tyndall and Huxley, and Farrar and Beecher were not around in those days. On the right was the dwelling of Mr. Graham, whose daughter Laura was once a teacher of mine. Her sister Mary, was a beautiful girl, and great favorite. Across the road from here, stood the school-house, and next lived Mr. Hubbard, a merchant: opposite Hubbard's lived our good Doctor Allen. What a wonderful vehicle to us boys was that two wheeled "*shays*" of his. He had three children, Joseph, Lucretia and Louisa: the latter a black-eyed beauty. Just beyond his house was a narrow ravine, deep as Tartarus, the sides covered with apple trees in full bearing. Just beyond lived " Uncle" Jabe Brooks, who had no children. Next to him was the house of Rev. Mr. Clarke, a graduate of Williams College. Elijah Thayer was his classmate: born in Buckland in 1795, and dying in 1824. He was one of the best Greek scholars of his day. Next to Hubbard's was his store, where the farmers' eggs and butter were exchanged for brown sugar and tea. Beyond, a blacksmith shop and a small house, and then, upon an eminence, stood the fine brick residence of Mr. Griswold. One of his sons, Wayne Griswold, was a distinguished physician, and prominent citizen of this State, and died at Circleville, Ohio, a few years since. Some little ways beyond this, lived Uncle "Alf"

Brooks, the richest man of the town, and the father of seventeen children. Let the Yankee couples of Massachusetts follow his example, if they would not see the state overrun with foreigners. He sent two sons to Amherst, and was much envied by us, poor boys, for his great wealth. I have since learned that he was worth about $4,000.

In those days, as most of the people came from a distance to church, we had a short intermission of half an hour between services, consequently everybody carried a lunch. In the fall and winter, Graham's, Dr. Allen's and "Uncle" Jabe's, were the favorite places of eating it, since there we were always furnished with apples, and at "Uncle" Jabe's with nice cider. "Uncle" Jabe was much beloved. Plain and simple and scanty was our fare in those days; and, yet, we had one dish that the whole West can't equal. "Ryeandingin" bread, made of rye flour and Indian meal, not sifted at the mill, but at home, kneaded for a whole hour, baked in iron skillets, placed in a brick oven at three o'clock in the afternoon, and not taken out till the next morning; it was bread fit for the gods.

By the way, Deacon Porter brought the first barrel of wheat flour to Buckland about 1829. Gathering and buying a quantity of chestnuts and walnuts, he took them to Troy, and exchanged them for flour. He was never tired of telling nor we of hearing of the wonders of that far off city. One of the great wonders was the ferry boats propelled by horse power, throwing into the shade the wooden horse of ancient Troy. Indeed the Deacon's story was more interesting to the boy, than Schleiman's story of his excavations to the man. But I am getting garrulous, yet young enough to stop with my tenth sheet.

Please give my respects to all who remember me, and believe me

Truly Yours,     B. WHITE.

Rev. William W. Johnson, of Greenfield, Wisconsin, sent as his contribution to the Centennial a book entitled "Records of the Descendants of David Johnson, of Leominster," a work of no little value to the Johnsons of Buckland, and which is to be kept in the town for reference.

Senator Winn preceded the regular toasts of the afternoon with a tribute to the sturdy race who came to Buckland a century ago, not finding it as to-day, but an unbroken forest. They created wealth, felled the timber and drove the Indian away. Among other things they fought against were bad habits, and here the speaker referred to the drinking propensities of the olden time when the ministers even set an example of tippling. The old Elder in Whitingham, in his father's day, on one occasion, closed the benediction by asking the Lord for mercy, grace and peace, and without a pause informed the people that a barrel of new rum had been received at his house, and he invited all to come over and partake of it. The fathers in Buckland were not ignorant for they read the law and discussed constitutional questions in town meeting. They had a stern theology but successful villiany never found a foothold here.

A sentiment was given for the old men of Buckland, and Dea. Silas Trowbridge of Buckland was called upon to respond. He believed that the good seed sown by the temperate, industrious and religious fathers of Buckland would bear good fruit in after generations. He had spent the whole of his long life within the limits of the town. The next toast was to the young men of Buckland, and Charles E. Ward was called out as their spokesman. He quoted the maxim: Old men for counsel young men for war, but the gathering of the day was one of peace, and the young soldier had no right in the "vet's" place at the camp-fire, and he would be contented to be a listener. He referred poetically to the winding Clesson, the burden of whose song is forward and not back—which might be adopted as a symbol of our future.

George D. Crittenden responded for "Our Town Officers." He compared the habits and manners of the people of to-day with those of the past. In olden time there were always two or three men in town who stood head and shoulders above their fellow-citizens. The Squire, the Deacon and the Minister were the law and the gospel. Now the average man is given a share in political and public affairs. To illustrate his point he told the following anecdote: Years ago a party of Buckland people settled on the Holland Purchase, 300 miles west of here, in she state of New York. Years afterwards a Buckland man went out there and they asked him who was the first Selectman in town, and he replied, "John Porter." "Who is your Deacon?" was the next question, and the answer was, "John Porter." "Who leads your choir?" "John Porter." "Who is Superintendent of your Sabbath-school?" "John Porter." "Who is Justice of the Peace?" "John Porter." "Who commands the militia company?" "John Porter." "Who did you send to the Legislature last year?" "John Porter." Out of patience, the next question was, "For heaven's sake, who made you?" And promptly came the response, "John Porter." People of the present day are far more independent in thought and action. The speaker, however, gave all honor to the sturdy men who founded a church without a bishop and a state without a king.

Edwin A. Davis was called upon in behalf of "Our Mechanics," and Hugo Mann was asked to speak for "Our Adopted Citizens," but these gentlemen could not be found. Dr. Josiah Trow, however, was said to be always on hand and ready, and came gallantly to the defence of the Medical profession. He gave the names of Buckland's physicians, commencing with Dr. Holbrook, in 1800. Dr. Allen was a famous man in his day and went into politics as well as medicine, and the speaker gave some anecdotes of his career in Buckland. His successors were Drs. Long, Ashley and the two Trows. Fourteen physicians had originated in town—more than was claimed by any other profession. Dr. Trow graphically described the old time practice of bleeding and dosing with calomel, and gave the following as the requisites for a successful practitioner in these days: He must be good looking—a handsome man: must have a foreign appearance; wear a ring; carry a cane and soft soap enough for a whole neighborhood, and then if possessing an abundance of cheek he might commence the study of medicine.

Rev. C. L. Guild was asked to speak in behalf of the clergy. Although not long a resident he was glad to be called upon as a Buckland clergyman. In 94 years the town had had five pastors—the speaker being the sixth. There was not a black mark against any of them. They had done their work well and so were well remembered. Pleasant anecdotes of Father Spaulding were given. Buckland had sent out many young men who had become ministers, and one was referred to who was soon to follow.

Rev. Samuel S. Clark of Holyoke responded to the toast to the women of Buckland, and took occasion to pay a tribute to Miss Mary Lyon, who had been an inmate of his father's house.

To Prof. W. F. Sherwin was given the closing toast—The Music and Musicians of Olden Times. He thought the audience had already had more toast than they could digest, and he would defer his speech until the next centennial. He, however, took occasion to recall the "old meeting-house"—not the "church," which he defined as an organization of believers—with its square galleries and sounding board; and he told how he feared and revered the minister; and of the singing circles at James B. Taylor's, not forgetting little incidents and anecdotes which were told in a happy vein that put the weary audience in the best humor. And thus the good times closed with Auld Lang Syne, Prof. Sherwin leading the singing and all joining in the grand old song.

Great credit is due the Committee for the day's success, and to the officers in charge who were prompt in carrying out the programme. The Shelburne Falls Band also needs a good word, for the music was one of the pleasant features of the occasion. Buckland is to be congratulated, and may her next centennial be as bright and joyous as that of 1879.

# The Buckland of a Century.

*Written for the Buckland Centennial Celebration, Sept. 10, 1879.*

BY REV. W. A. NICHOLS.

Hail! present citizens of Buckland, hail!
Both you who till the soil, and dig for gold
One furrow deep, where lies the primal wealth
Of States and empires old, and sinews of
The Commonwealths in future to arise:
And you who toil in shops as artisans,
Or build in architecture simple or
Elaborate, the homes of other men,
And rear the temples of the living God;
And you who buy and sell the products of
An honest toil, which yields you wholesome gain;
And you who teach the young idea how
To shoot into proportions full and strong;
And you who preach the words of life to men;
And you who practice in the healing art
To make men whole, nor multiply their ills;
And you who doctor men with civil law
To heal their strife, nor make them strive the more;
In answer to your hearty call we come
From East and West, from North and South, from
  homes
Which we have found both far and near, to homes
And friends and kindred dear which we had left,
And some of us to pay our compliments
Unto the dear old mountains and the steep
Side-hills—to course once more your rivulet
In which we've often plunged at noon-tide hour,
To thread your tiny brooks, which babble not
So loud as when we strayed along their banks
To toss the speckled trout on rainy days,
Too wet for decent folks to work out doors;
We come to contemplate with you, the course
Of time—the ways of men and providence
Of God, in this good town a hundred years.

II.—THIS TOWN A HUNDRED YEARS AGO.

Until one hundred years ago,
As civil history will show,
These hills, these dales and streams, for want
Of name, were part of Charlemont.
This *Buckland*, where, we surely know,
Did also roam the timid doe,
Was mostly wilderness profound,
Where native wildness did abound,
The wolf did prowl at dead of night,
The panther's scream did so affright
The mother in the cabin drear,
That husband's footsteps at the door,
Gave joy she never felt before.
The bear did guard her hollow tree,
And thus defend her family.
  The red man left these woods in quest
Of better hunting farther west;
And frontier settlers then were rare,
With dwellings scattered here and there;
In the deep wood a house appearing,
Surrounded by a little clearing.
The weary huntsman climbed your mountains,
And slaked his thirst at gushing fountains,
Until the sweet and tender venison
Was carried home, a precious benison.
The bridle paths, like Indian trails,
Led o'er these hills and through the vales;
From settlement to settlement,
The pioneer on horseback went,
Or drawn by oxen through the snow,
With plodding steps, full sure, but slow;
Yet pioneers were seldom sad;
Their homes were merry, hearthstones glad,
Except when suddenly alarmed,

They feared their household would be harmed.
If neighbors then were far away,
Too far to visit every day,
'Twas rare that loneliness was felt,
Though few and far between they dwelt.
Too busy in their household plans,
Too active with their heads and hands:
No modes had they of modern sort,
For killing time to make it short;
And when the people came together,
In sunny or in stormy weather,
Right social times were there, I'm sure,
And better far for being fewer.
Then lads and lasses long apart,
With cheerful flow of loving heart,
Would congregate in joyous bands:
By tasting lips and shaking hands,
Despite the rural life they led,
Would prove that Cupid was not dead.

The otter, and the crafty mink,
Along your crystal river's brink,
Gained not their food by simply wishing—
They lived by industry—in fishing.
The nimble salmon leaped your falls,
And skilful boys made lusty hauls,
Where grown up trout, in places deep,
Could not their hiding places keep.

The times were rough, the country new,
And sluggard life, as now, was blue,
Because the acres would not yield
Where none would work to till the field.
Yet industry, as now, was crowned
With golden harvests from the ground,
Made soft by sweat in patient toil;
'Tis this that fructifies the soil,
In countries old and countries new;
So I believe and so must you.

III.—THE CONQUEST OF INDUSTRY DURING THE
FIRST FIFTY YEARS.

How great the work of pioneers,—
But little do they know
Who reap the fruit in after years,
Without their work to do.

The stately mansion, broad and high,
Impression makes profound:
But never tells th· passer by
The work of underground;

What ma sive stones at the foundation!
What toil to place them there!
All which is needful preparation
To rear the structure fair.

So when a hundred years have finished
The work long since begun,
Rude ob·tacles are so diminished,
That farming is but fun.

The woodman's ax, the falling trees,
In solitude profound,
With stroke and crash upon the breeze,
Echo the forest round,

Until the forest monarchs lie,
By acres on the ground,
And there are left with sun to dry,
Till burning time comes round;

When, through the country far and wide
Under the blazing sun,
Dark smoke betrays the rolling tide
Of *burning* now begun.

During those long and sultry days,
In which the dog-star rages,
The country through was in a blaze
For farms, in future ages.

After the reaper's task was done,
And harvest home was sung,

The work of chopping up came on,
  The seared logs among.

Next, piling logs came on full soon:
  If corn was ripe for toasting,
The black-faced boys by light of moon
  Had jolly times at roasting.

This work of which you now are hearing
  So full of smut and health,
In ancient phrase was called a "clearing"—
  Grandfather's way to wealth.

Thus fields continued nearing,
  Till clearing touched to clearing:
  And men of common sense
Did lean on the line fence,
And freely talk together,
About the crops and weather.
Then housewives more at ease,
Of butter talked and cheese:
Hence, friendly gossip grew,
To tell of something new,
And add a little more
To what was told before.
  The postman next to view
Appeared, with much of new:
Not in express by steam,
(A fact not then in dream)
But on a jaded nag,
Bundle in saddle bag,
Did wind his horn to tell
What the wide world befell.
A famous man was he,
As bustling man could be.

And many-other things were done,
  (The people then were strong)
Which now are freely left alone,
  By aged and by young.

The fields, of stone, both great and small
  Were cleared for better tilling;
With lines of long and rough stone wall
  The country then was filling.

I've lifted stone on that old farm,
  Till I saw stars by day:
And yet it never did me harm—
  I'd rather work than play.

An orchard on the steep side hill,
  Or somewhere else about,
And not far off a cider mill,
  Were needful fitting out.

The still-worm was a constant bore,
  And very hard to kill.
When thirst was ever craving more,
  And more would never fill.

Ah! there were some of noble blood,
  Yes! they were truly braves,
To conquer fields and fell the wood,
  But rank themselves as slaves.

In revolutionary day
  This goodly town was born,
And after that, was war with Shay,—
  Whom justice brands with scorn.

Strong-minded woman then was here:
  And woman's rights were rife:—
Woman, who rarely knew a fear,
  Yet faithful as a wife.

Gaunt war had sucked the nation's blood,
  And thinned the volunteers:
At home, there was a lack of food,
  But not of woman's cheers.

Then, mothers often went afield,
  To keep the boys in train:
When harvests to her sickle yield,
  They save the precious grain:

She lent the sire to freedom's cause,
  And took his place at home:
'Twas thus she broke oppression's laws,
  For ages yet to come.

She had a right to wear the crown
  Of Ceres on the farm:
And ever after reap renown
  Where valor is the charm.

These fifty years of tug and Lold,
  To conquer virgin soil,

Called for a people strong and bold,
　To grapple with the toil.

## IV.—THE MEN AND WOMEN OF LONG AGO.

*Wards* were first upon the soil,
First in strokes of hardy toil;
Miller John, an upright soul,
Left the grist and took the toll.
*Taylors* next in order came;
Many people bore this name:
Samuel stood up and cried
Who next here should be a bride.
Othniel among the pines,
Built a park for stags and hinds;
William's meadow often made
Ample common for parade.
Lemuel, until quite old,
In the church did office hold.
See Enos, never fond of strife,
A friendly neighbor all his life.
Levi as a quiet man,
Lived by rule and worked by plan.
*Sherwin*, as a deacon gifted,
With the pastor ever lifted.
Deacon *Pratt* lived near to God,—
Paths of love he ever trod.
*Carters*, always very neat,
Strove to make their works complete.
*Johnsons* lived as paradoxes,
Cutting stone and hunting foxes.
*Brooks* did ever farm it well,
Every passer by could tell.
*Griswold* was a thorough man,
Firm to execute his plan.
*Pomeroy* was an honored name,
Never widely known to fame.
*Hubbard*, thoughtful, taciturn,
Slow to speak and quick to learn.
*Putnams*, every one will say,
Dealing justly, showed fair play.
Those who knew the *Farnhams* well,
Can their fortunes better tell.
*Trowbridge*, Rufus had the skill
Funds to settle left by will.
*Ellis*, after urgent calls,
Helped a bridge across the falls.
*Ballard*, upright, fond of scrubbing,
Gave rough fields a thorough drubbing.
Many others we could show,
Had important work to do;
Doing well with hearty cheer,
Left a proof of being here.
Housework everywhere would tell,
Women lived their epics well:—
Carding wool and spinning flax,
Keeping floors as neat as wax,
Clothing sons and daughters warm,
'Gainst the chilling winter's storm.
For the daughter soon to wed,
Picking geese for feather bed;
Ever at the church on Sunday,
Washing up on every Monday.
　Saddle, pillion, pillow, three
Rode one horse, as you may see;
Saddle was the father's seat;
Pillion mother took behind;
(Moderns no such couple find;)
On a pillow baby rode,
At the pommel as it could.
On the Sabbath let us see
What of this ancient family;
At the seventh day's setting sun,
Of the week the work was done;
Playing now was desecration;
Social visits profanation;
Night began before the day,
Such was God's appointed way.

Sabbath day at half past ten,
All the women, boys and men,
Were expected in their pew
When the pastor came in view.
Pulpits then were perched on high,
Like a barrel in the sky;
Sounding board was higher still,
Which the preacher's voice might fill,
And convey the gospel sound
Freely all the flock around.
All the people stood in prayer;
None ever ventured sitting there;
Seats went up when people rose,
Helping them to find repose.
Prayer once over, bang! bang! bang!
All around, whang, whang, whang!
Fusillade of volunteers,
Falls not harsher on the ears.
　Churches then, for best of reasons,
Had no fire in winter seasons.
Best of sermons one could hear;
Long enough in cold severe.
Rapping toes upon the heel,
Much discomfort did reveal;
Better when the text began,
Did the children like Amen.
　Worship over none too soon,
All went out to spend the noon;
At the neighbor's roaring fire,
Sat the mother and the sire,

Taking comfort at their ease,
Freely ate their bread and cheese.
Brief the hour of intermission
To relieve the chilled condition;
Fortified with warmth and food,
They another chill withstood.
When this second close had come,
No time lost in getting home.
In the evening, by the fire,
Sat the children with the sire;
In that circle was no schism,
All must say the catechism.
　Modern folks are wont to smile
At a Sabbath in this style;
But I tell you all as one,
Sabbath then was thoroughly done;
Sabbath influence went then
Through the week with boys and men.
With no Sunday paper then,
Telling people where and when
Stocks would fall and grain would rise,
When to purchase merchandise,
Men acquired a competence,
Rarely suffered lack of pence.
Then it was no Yankee notion,
Leaving bail to cross the ocean,
From prison and disgrace to flee,
Hiding shame beyond the sea;
Franchise spurned the purchased vote,
Honor watched to pay the note.

　Of father Spaulding now a kindly word;
He first as pastor fed the people here;
As scholar, and with charge to keep the flock,
He faithful was and true, through heat and cold;
His words in social life were few, but well
Selected to convey the kindness of
A warm and loving heart. A little odd,
Through absent-mindedness he sometimes caused
A smile, soon checked, through reverence for the man.
His most emphatic gesture was to rise
On tiptoe, with clasped hands held up,
And face upturned, come down upon his heels
To add importance to his sentiment.
He died in eighteen hundred twenty-three
At spring-time, after a long winter of
Revival labor with his charge, full aged,—
At seventy-two. How old he seemed! how ripe!
And richly fruited for the Father's house.

　Young Abner Taylor was in college when
This swift winged century swept by the point
Half-way. In purpose old, and rich in thought,
His graduation two years past, when he
Was suddenly arrested; as the man
Who leaves the plough in furrow; just begun
The field before him left; where he had hoped
To sow and reap the later harvest full.
Delirium had siezed him in its wild
Embrace, that he saw neither earth nor heaven,
In its true light;—was neither here nor there;
Till soon his waning senses lost their power
To act. As some tall vessel anchored in
The storm and rocked by winds and waves upon
A rolling sea, affrights the men who stand
Upon the shore, without the power to help,
We thus did stand and view his agony;
Until the shattered bark went down beneath
The lethal wave, and left the spirit free
To soar away to him who gave it first,
And so it sometimes is, the good die first.

　John Porter was a man, all manhood to
The core, yet he could also be a boy,
When such would best befit the circumstance,
(A good boy to be sure, as all boys should be)
The object gained, he could put on the man
Again, and be as manly as before.

Such style of manhood best befits a world
Like this: for, so the Man in Holy Writ
Became all things unto all men, that he
Might gain the more from wrong to right.
To self-dependence left in early days,
He found a generous heart to take him in.
While youth was fresh, he joined the teachers' corps
In winter months, and Mary Lyon had
For buxom pupil, in her early teens.
As quick in thought and comprehensive in
His scope of men and things, more popular
None ever was within his sphere, nor need
Desire to be; and yet he ever turned
His popularity to usefulness.
The trusts committed to him, sacredly
He held. The office was the greater for
The officer who filled it full, and well.
As teacher of the youth, and leader in
The choir, and deacon of the church, as one
In military life,—selectman of
The town,—as legislative member of
The House, and privy councilor of State;
In one,—in all, he was at home, and served
The people and his country ever well.

As the last century drew near its close,
East side of Putnam's hill, a child was born,
Whose early thoughts were wont to swell beyond
The narrow precincts of her natal home;
That westward hill she often climbed, because
It overlooked, and down into the world.
Enthusiastic, and yet crude was her
Beginning; but the world which she looked out
Upon in childhood, was to feel, to its
Remotest bounds, her influence for good.
The hundred years which make this century,
And mark this joyous day centennial,
Had passed their middle point in twenty-nine;
And Mary Lyon then was thirty-two,
The crudities of early youth were gone.
She then had taught her schools in Graham's hall,
And more elsewhere. Her great ability
To mold and elevate the female mind
Was evident by proof beyond a doubt,
And, slowly, now, and surely she prepared
To meet her life-work face to face, and do
Her best. In thirty-seven the Holyoke school
Began. In twelve short years her work was done.
Yet through her pupils she is living still,
In every quarter of the globe; and on
The islands of the sea her voice is heard.

So perfect was her plan of school for girls
To meet a wide extended want, deep felt,
That, years revolving, do not wear it out
Of harmony with need; and the supply
Of patronage increases, ever, as
The years go by, to show the plan correct.
A thorough, deep and comprehensive view
Of female education; was, at first,
The source and spring of her great enterprise.
That *heart* should, equal, share with intellect,
In cultivation up to womanhood,
Was ever cardinal with her in thought.
And next to this was the *magnetic* power
Of her great soul in sympathy with those,
She led in toilsome progress up the hill.

As great in plan, less perfect in detail,
She wrought the system into *perfect* whole;
But gave details to others who could work
The parts with more facility than she.
One major-General, alone is found
Among ten thousand who may better do
The detailed work of a subordinate.
As chief commander, very few her peers;
None better knew than she, to choose her aids.
Within these facts, may often be concealed
The secret of a great and useful life.

## V.—THE BOYS AND GIRLS OF THE OLDEN TIME.

If I can tell you nothing new,
I sure will tell you what was true
Of the boys and girls of the days of yore;
Please this receive and nothing more.
The boys of sixty years ago,
Were much the same as boys are now.
The men, now woven into rhyme,
Were simply boys in olden time.
And ladies now in caps and glasses,
Were gleesome maidens; bonny lasses.
Then youthful blood did have its frolic,
If not by rule then sure by rollick:
If boys were fonder then of sliding,
Girls liked as well, the fun of riding
On goodly hand-sled drawn by boys,
And, in the sport made equal noise.
When one has said whate'er he can,
"The child was father of the man."
As that was true so was this other;
The girl was stepping-stone to mother.
The elder boys dressed flax, you know,
Girls in their teens were spinning tow;
Were also taught to use the broom,
And how to practice in the loom,
Which played the tune of how to thrive;
Thus home was busy as a hive,
Where drones to working bees must turn,
And eat the honey which they earn.
The public schools in early days,
Contained but little we can praise.
Geography was too abstruse,
Until Mary Lyon taught its use,
And grammar was as strange as Greek,
In teaching people how to speak.
In mathematics, *boys* must be
Proficient to the rule of three.
But girls, as scholars passed right well,
If they could read and write and spell.
If any wished to enter college,
These must forsooth, extend their knowledge.
The pastor, then, in requisition,
Was put, to fit for this position.
In composition, letter writing
Furnished practice for inditing.
If parents then had better known
"Man shall not live by bread alone,"
That human bodies are but shells,
In which the higher nature dwells,
That after the Creator's plan,
Mind is the measure of the man.
Their sons and daughters then had found
Means for improvement more profound,
If less of muscle more of thought,
More comprehension would have brought;
But *who* could tell, when no one knew,
The parts that lacked, or, what to do?
Step by step improvement grows;
And if, perchance, some wise one knows
Two steps ahead to take at once,
He is for this pronounced a dunce,
Not suitable to show the way;
And would most surely lead astray.
He went too fast, as people said;
None, sure, would follow *where he led*.
Yet such as these must lead the van;
And higher progress ever plan;
Where nobler spirits first have gone,
Slow creeping thought may follow on;
Yet looking back for forward motion,
Like ships stern foremost on the ocean,
Not e'en stern foremost will those move
Until in practice you shall prove,
By demonstration plain as day,
Which is for them the better way.
And, when you've made the case so plain,

They cannot help advantage gain,
They overlook their good adviser,
And thank themselves for being wiser.

## VI.—SOME OF THE CHANGES OF REVOLVING YEARS.

On every hand the truth appears,
That in these swift revolving years,
The world has moved at equal rate
No thing retains its former state.
The coach and four for locomotion,
Is but an antiquated notion,
An iron kettle full of steam,
Is better far than four horse team ;
The post to telegraph gives place :
This vies with lightning in the race
Of taking news to utmost bound
Of human habitation found.
What though the world through these seem
        smaller?
Humanity is so much taller,
To overlook both things and men :
And better know the where and when,
    Your hill-sides have washed and washed
        again
By oft repeated summer rain,
Have given to the fields below,
Where still you plough and plant and sow,
Their virgin fatness to that soil,
Where you more easily can toil :
And make the fewer acres yield,
The harvests of a larger field.
    On hill tops once your pasture ground,
Returning forests will be found :
This second growth will moisture bring
To feed again the failing spring ;
And wood, as better crop than grain,
The primal value will sustain.
This take as nature's form of fallow
To reimburse your soil, made shallow.
On fewer acres, greater skill,
The barn more readily will fill :
And better tools will supersede
Some of the hands which now you need.
These super-numeraries send,
Far westward, where their skill can lend
Unto the hardy pioneer,
Now toiling on our broad frontier,
Your Yankee skill from Pilgrim land.
Then ruder men will understand
The way to do, with least, the best,
(Too oft a secret in the West)
And they will teach, as well they can,
How *you* can make a broader plan ;
And when these secrets are found out,
Both will be Yankees, *lengthened out*.
For, when, with this expanded view,
It is seen what saving things will do,
With ample means, both sooner can
Fill to the brim the larger plan.
What though a hundred years you boast
Hard by New England's rocky bound coast?
New England's equal self has gone,
Much further towards the setting sun :
To be the frame-work of the nation,
And underlie its broad foundation.
High up among the Rocky Mountains
Where fortunes flow from golden fountains,
And o'er the vast extended plains
Of prairie land, are Yankee brains.
New England's thrifty sons and daughters
Surge along Pacific waters,
Where freedom-truth, a soul do fill,
There's Plymouth Rock and Bunker Hill.

*Metcalf & Company, Printers, Northampton.*